Ruby's SO Rude

First published in 2013 by Wayland
Text © Wayland 2013
Illustrations © Jack Hughes 2013

Wayland
338 Euston Road
London NW1 3BH

Wayland Australia
Level 17/207 Kent Street
Sydney, NSW 2000

Commissioning Editor: Victoria Brooker
Design: Lisa Peacock and Alyssa Peacock

British Library Cataloguing in Publication Data
Heneghan, Judith.
Ruby's SO rude. -- (Dragon School)
1. Etiquette--Pictorial works--Juvenile fiction.
2. Children's stories--Pictorial works.
I. Title II. Series III. Hughes, Jack.
823.9'2-dc23

ISBN 978 0 7502 7958 1

Printed in China

Wayland is a division of Hachette Children's Books,
an Hachette UK Company
www.hachette.co.uk

Ruby's SO Rude

Written by Judith Heneghan
Illustrated by Jack Hughes

WAYLAND

Ruby and her friends were going on a picnic.

They all felt excited about their day out in the forest.
Sometimes, however, Ruby forgot her manners.

'Please can you pass me my backpack, Ruby?'
asked Jasmine.
  'Get it yourself!' said Ruby, rudely.
She pushed past and took off into the sky.

'Hey, wait for us!' cried Brandon.
But Ruby wasn't listening.

The young dragons flew over the treetops.
'Wow!' said Noah, peering through
his binoculars. 'What an amazing butterfly!'

'Where?' said Ruby. 'Let me see!'
She reached forward and grabbed
the binoculars for herself.

'Don't be rude, Ruby,' said Noah. 'You should ask before you take something that isn't yours.'

'Oh, who cares about that?' said Ruby,
flapping her wings.

'I do,' sighed Noah, sadly.

The sun shone brightly through the trees.
Jasmine flew down to the ground.
She wanted to put on her new sun hat.

'I never wear a sun hat!' said Ruby.

'Sun hats are for babies.'

'That's a rude thing to say,' said Jasmine.

'I don't care,' replied Ruby, sticking out her tongue.

Jasmine felt hurt, though. She put her sun hat away.

The dragons were beginning to feel hungry.
They looked for a place to have their picnic.
Then Brandon saw a shady spot on
the other side of a stream.

'Ooh look, stepping stones!' he said. 'Much more fun than flying! Let's jump across them, one at a time!'

But Ruby didn't wait for Brandon to cross first.
She pushed him out of the way.
Brandon slipped and fell
into the water.

'Why didn't you say "excuse me"?' complained Brandon. 'Now I'm all wet!' He felt annoyed. Ruby was SO rude!

Ruby, however, wasn't bothered.
   'Last one across is a dragon dropping!' she shouted,
hopping over to the other side. She sat down on
a log underneath a tree. 'I'm starving!'

Before the others could catch her up, she opened her lunchbox and took out a big cheesy rock burger.

Ruby was too busy munching to see the slithery snake above her head. But the slithery snake saw Ruby's rock burger.

'Watch out, Ruby!' called Noah, as the snake swung down, pushed her out of the way and snatched the rock burger right out of her hand.

Ruby looked up in surprise. Now the snake was coiled back around its branch, eating her lunch!

The snake didn't look very sorry. Instead it stuck out its tongue and dropped some cheesy crumbs on her head.

'You are SO RUDE!' yelled Ruby, feeling hurt
and sad and annoyed all at the same time.
'Now I've got nothing to eat! You should
learn some manners!'

By this time, the other dragons
had caught up with Ruby. They
all stared up at the naughty snake.
Then Jasmine started giggling.

'What's so funny?' asked Ruby. Then she realised that she'd been behaving just like the snake! Soon, all four dragons were laughing.

'I'm sorry I've been so rude,' she said. 'I didn't mean to hurt anyone's feelings. From now on, I'm going to be really polite.'

Suddenly, her tummy rumbled.
She peeked into Brandon's lunchbox.
It was full of lovely things to eat.

'Would you like to share some of my lunch?' asked Brandon.
'Yes please,' said Ruby, gratefully. 'Thank you very much.'

Meet all the Dragons— Brandon, Jasmine, Noah and Ruby!

978 0 7502 7959 8

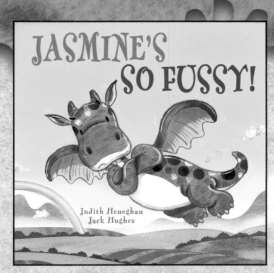

978 0 7502 7961 1

978 0 7502 7960 4

978 0 7502 7958 1

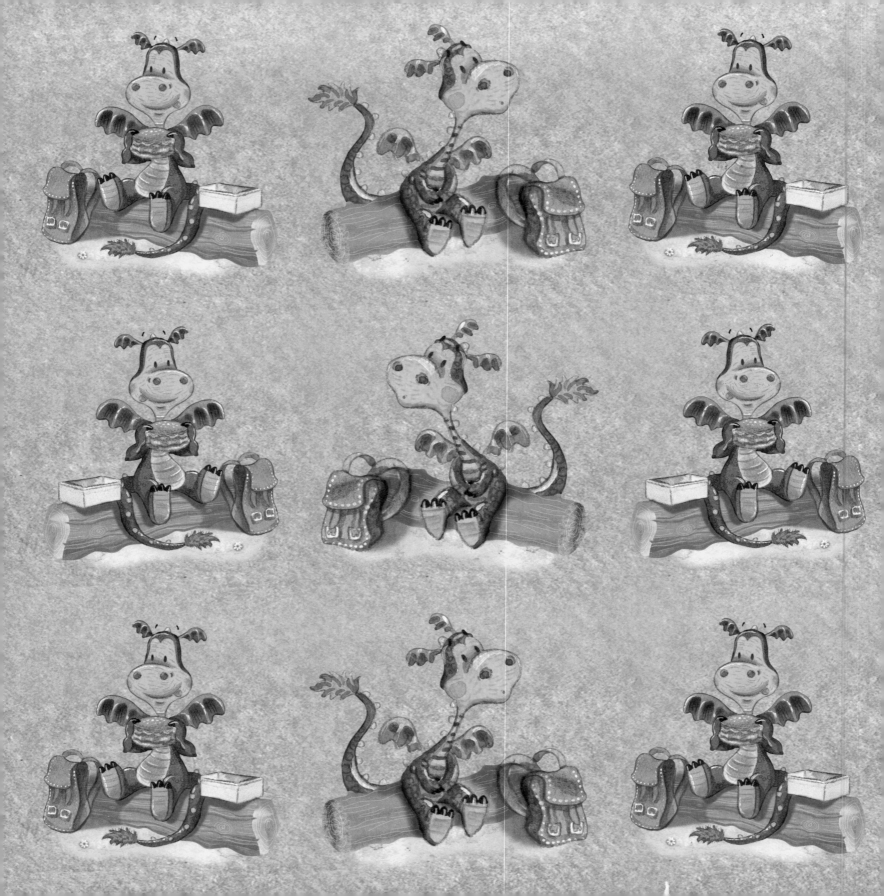